10 9 8 7 6 5 4 3

Library of Congress Cataloging-in-Publication Data
St. Germain, Mark
Three Cups/Mark St. Germain: Illustrated by April Willy

p. cm.

Summary: *Three Cups* teaches children, from an early age, the rewards of practicing
a timeless, unique and effective method of personal financial management and charity.
(1. Savings-Fiction 2. Stewardship-Fiction 3. Financial management for children-Fiction
4. Charity for children) I. Willy, April, ill. III Title.

LCCN:2008911284
ISBN: 978-0-9794563-0-5

Printed in China

The illustrations in this book were executed in acrylic on masonite board.
The type was set in Garamond Premier Pro.

Concept for the book *Three Cups* and book design by Scott Willy

www.3cupsbook.com

For *all* families.

On my fifth birthday,
my parents gave me a wonderful present.

They promised it would take me on many adventures.

"These three cups are from our cupboard," I said.
"Is *this* my present?"

"There's more," my mother explained.
"Look inside the envelope."

"We think it's time you started getting a weekly allowance," my father told me. "And every year it will grow bigger, just like you will."

"Every week we will help you divide your allowance among the three cups," Mother said. "One cup is for *savings*, one cup is for *spending*, and one cup is for *charity*."

After we discussed how to divide the money and put it in the cups, we put them in my room.

"But what about the adventures?" I asked.
"They'll come," my father promised.

Every Saturday, week after week, I got excited
when it was time to put my allowance into the three cups.

Every Sunday, Monday, Tuesday, Wednesday, Thursday
and Friday... I forgot about the money.

One day my mother said, "It looks to me like your cups are filling up. Let's see how much you have."

She helped me count. I was surprised at how much there was, especially in my Savings Cup.

"I have an idea," Mother said. "Let's take a trip to the bank."

"You're rich!" said my sister.

"I think I want to keep saving my allowance in cups," I told my mother.

"You can do that," she said. "But let's ask Mr. Duncan how the bank can help you save even more."

Mr. Duncan was the president of the bank.

He told me he could keep my money safe and
make it grow. I asked him how.

He said that when I put my money in his bank,
it would be called a "deposit." It would be placed in my
very own savings account, which would hold my money
for me just like my Savings Cup did.

Best of all, Mr. Duncan said the bank would pay me
to keep my money there! The money the bank pays is
called "interest." He explained to me how it works.

"Interest" sounded interesting to me.

After I deposited the money from my Savings Cup,
Mr. Duncan gave me a lollipop.

I asked for one for my sister, too.

"Is this the adventure?" I asked Mother.
"It's just the beginning. Do you know how much money
you have in your Spending Cup?" she asked.

After we got home from the bank, I counted the money in my Spending Cup. I wanted to buy a new baseball glove, but I knew I hadn't saved enough yet.

"Do you really want that glove?" Mother asked.

"I do," I told her.

Mother said if I just saved my money for a little while longer, I'd have enough to buy it.

"You could buy a doll instead," my sister said.

So, I waited for one week, then two, then three. By then, I had more than enough to buy my new baseball glove.

I bought my sister a present with the money left over.

"This is an adventure," I told my mother and father.
"It's not over yet," Father said. "What about your Charity Cup?"

Charity means helping others. But there were so many people
who needed help, and my Charity Cup was so small.

I went to my parents and asked them what I could do.

"A hundred things," Father said.

"A hundred times a hundred things," Mother told me.

Then I remembered that my school was collecting food
for needy families. I asked my mother if I could go
with her to the grocery store. With the money from
my Charity Cup, I bought eight cans of soup.

When I brought them to my teacher, Miss Phillips,
she asked me if I would like to help deliver
all the food our school collected.

The families we helped were happy to receive our gifts.
Helping them made me feel happy, too.

That night my father asked which cup was my favorite.

"My Spending Cup," I said. "No, my Savings Cup.
But my Charity Cup made me feel good, too."

*"Saving, Spending and Charity," Father told me.
"Doing all three things as you keep growing up...
that's the adventure."*

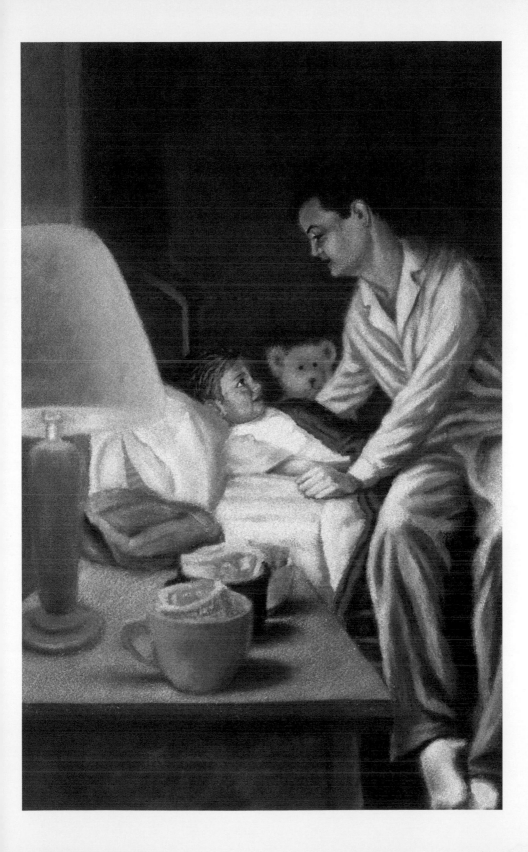

The weeks went by.
Every week I divided my allowance into my three cups.

The years went by.
Every year my allowance grew.

When I got my first job, mowing our neighbor's yard,
I also put the money I made into my three cups.

By the time I was in high school I had bought many things
with money from my Spending Cup.

With the money from my Charity Cup,
I helped many people.

And when I graduated from high school,
I used money from my savings account at the bank to
help pay for the college I went to.

I packed my three cups to take with me.

Today my own son turned five years old.

"Happy Birthday," I said.

"Are you ready for an adventure?"

Parent's Guide:
Getting started with *Three Cups*.

Above all else, enjoy the *Three Cups* Adventure you'll share with your children. Remember, it's not how much money one has, but rather how one uses it that really matters. *Three Cups* will help establish good habits in your children, and they can continue to build on them as they grow older.

1. Pick a special day to begin: a birthday, a holiday or another notable occasion.

2. Agree on how much your children should receive for their allowance on a weekly basis.

3. Decide (for now) how that allowance should be divided among the Savings, Spending and Charity Cups.

4. Read *Three Cups* to your children, or ask them to read it to you. Talk about the book and answer any questions they may have. Explain that *Three Cups* is a wonderful adventure, but it is also a responsibility that you, and your children, are committing to.

5. Choose three different cups from your cupboard. Label each accordingly with the words: "Savings", "Spending" and "Charity". You might also help your children decorate their cups to make them unique and more personal.

6. Designate a safe place for the three cups; be there to help and watch your children divide their allowance money among the three cups each week, especially as you are first getting started.

7. Discuss with your children some of the things they want to save for. Encourage them to make a "wish list" of things they may use their Spending Cup money for. Talk with them about who they would like to help with their Charity Cup. Together, research what charitable activities your children want to learn about by using the local phone book, the Internet or speaking with individuals from your school, church or other civic organizations.

8. Once your children have become accustomed to dividing their allowance and the cups begin to fill, agree on a good time to bring your children and their accumulated Savings Cup money to the bank.

9. During your first visit to the bank, ask a bank representative to allow your children to observe the opening of their account and encourage them to ask any questions they may have.

10. As your children grow older, continue your dialogue with them about what they hope to do with their savings, spending and charity funds. As your children's ambitions and interests change, the percentages of their allowance they put in each cup might also change. Encourage them, as their savings account grows, to discuss other banking options and services with your bank or other financial industry professionals.

We hope you have been touched by this book
and it will encourage you to introduce your children,
grandchildren, nieces, nephews, and others
to the Three Cups program.

When you do, they are sure to have many memorable
adventures that others will enjoy hearing about.
We have a special section on our Web site reserved
for these inspiring stories. Simply visit:

www.3cupsbook.com/share

All of us have the opportunity to make a difference
in our families, communities and in the world at large.

After reading this book, we think you'll agree
it's as easy as one, two three.